IMAGINE THAT

Licensed exclusively to Imagine That Publishing Ltd
Tide Mill Way, Woodbridge, Suffolk, IP12 1AP, UK
www.imaginethat.com
Copyright © 2020 Imagine That Group Ltd
All rights reserved
2 4 6 8 9 7 5 3 1
Manufactured in China

Written by Kitty Taylor
Illustrated by Gabi Murphy

ISBN 978-1-78958-587-2

A catalogue record for this book is available from the British Library

Little Bunny's Home Time

Kitty Taylor and
Gabi Murphy

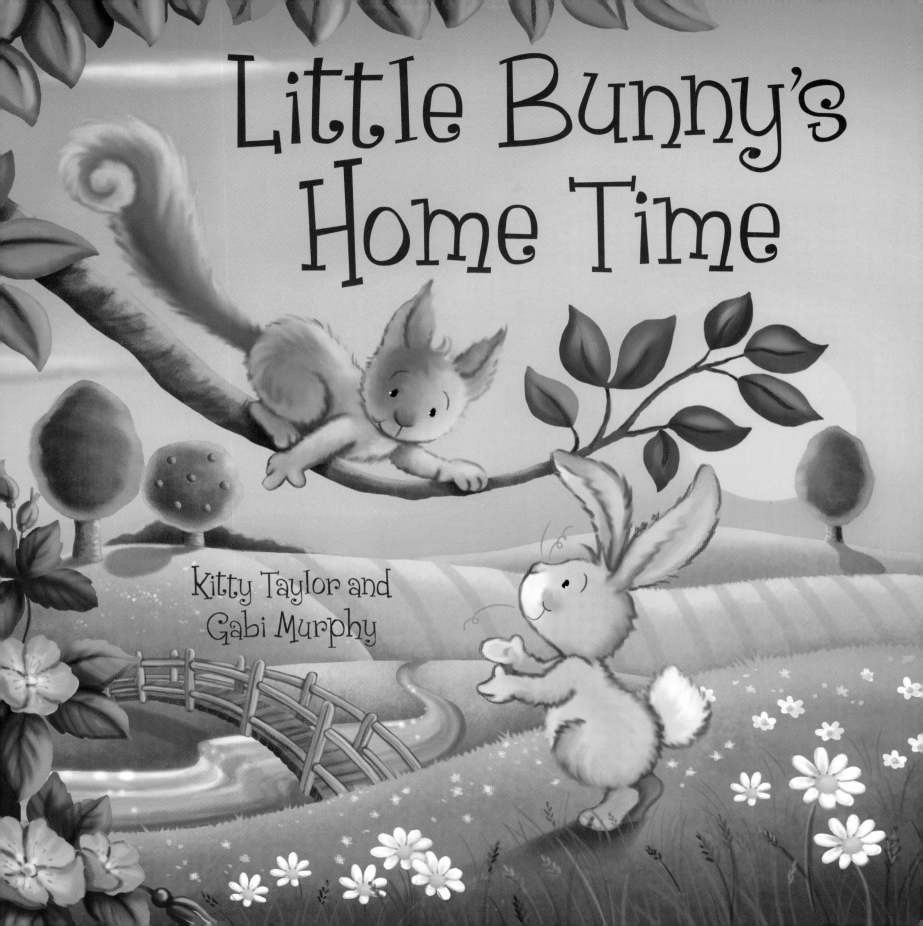

Little Bunny peeped out of his burrow under the apple tree. It was a hot, sunny day – just right for playing.

'Don't play too late!' called Mummy Bunny as Little Bunny hopped, skipped and scampered away. 'It's home time when the sun goes down behind the trees.'

Little Bunny hopped, skipped and scampered to the vegetable patch.

First, he stopped to nibble the sweet green lettuces. Then he chased the butterflies up and down the rows of carrots.

Next, Little Bunny squeezed under the gate and hopped, skipped and scampered out into the meadow.

He did somersaults, cartwheels and handsprings in the long summer grass.

Little Bunny hopped, skipped and scampered to the bridge that crossed a little stream.

He picked up some sticks and dropped them into the water. Then he ran to the other side of the bridge to see which stick came out first. He did it again and again!

Little Bunny crossed the bridge and hopped, skipped and scampered up the hill where he spotted some big rocks.

'Great for jumping on!' said Little Bunny to himself. And he jumped from rock to rock, all the way up the hill.

At the top of the hill, Little Bunny hopped, skipped and scampered into the woods. He played hide-and-seek with the bees in the trees.

Little Bunny was so busy playing that he didn't notice the sun starting to go down behind the trees. It was his home time … and he was LOST!

The first animal that Little Bunny saw was Deer.
'Hello, Deer. It's my home time, but I can't
remember where 'home' is. Can you help?'

'Follow the path to Owl's house, with a red door,'
said Deer. 'He will help you.'

So Little Bunny followed the path until he came to two trees, each with a coloured door. But which was the red one? Little Bunny had a big think and picked one.

'Hello, Owl,' said Little Bunny when Owl opened his door. 'It's my home time, but I can't remember where 'home' is. Can you help?'

'Find the path that goes down the hill, not up,' said Owl. 'You will see Squirrel's tree. She will help you.'

Soon, Little Bunny found two paths.
But which way was up and which way was down?
He had a big think and picked one.

'Hello, Squirrel!' he called when Squirrel appeared on a branch. 'It's my home time, but I can't remember where 'home' is. Can you help?'

'Cross the bridge and follow the stream to a meadow full of daisies,' said Squirrel. 'Fox lives there. He will help you.'

Soon, Little Bunny came across two meadows. But which one was full of daisies? He had another big think and picked one.

'Hello, Fox!' he called when he spotted Fox in the long summer grass. 'It's my home time, but I can't remember where 'home' is. Can you help?'

'Find the gate with a 3 on it,' said Fox. 'Mouse lives there. He will help you.'

At last, Little Bunny came to a wall with gates in it.
But which one was number 3? '1 … 2 … 3 … found it!'
shouted Little Bunny excitedly.

'Hello, Mouse!' he said when he heard Mouse squeaking. 'It's my home time, but I can't remember where 'home' is. Can you help?'

'Hop through the carrots,' said Mouse. 'When you get to the apple tree, look down!'

As the last rays of sunshine went down behind the trees, Little Bunny spotted the apple tree, with his burrow beneath it. He was home!

Little Bunny was so tired that he fell asleep at dinner. 'Goodnight, Little Bunny,' said Mummy Bunny, gently carrying him to bed. 'It'll soon be time for another busy day.'

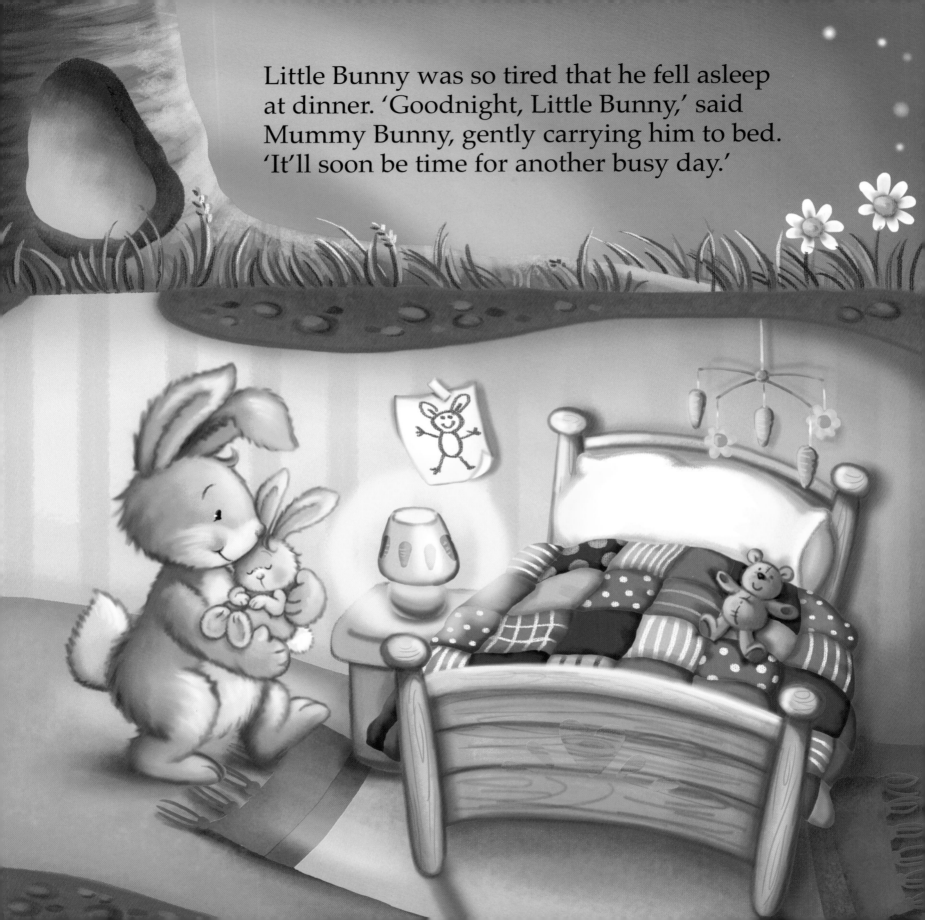